OTHER YOUNG YEARLING BOOKS YOU WILL ENJOY:

Stick-in-the-Mud Turtle

LILLIAN HOBAN

A Young Yearling Book

Published by
Dell Publishing
a division of
Bantam Doubleday Dell Publishing Group, Inc.
666 Fifth Avenue
New York, New York 10103

ISBN: 0-440-40622-6

Reprinted by arrangement with William Morrow & Co., Inc., on behalf of Greenwillow Books

Printed in the United States of America

May 1992

10 9 8 7 6 5 4 3 2 1

WES

For Ginger

HA HAMUD YOTER MI
SHNAY HA KLAVIM

Once there was
a turtle named Fred.
He lived with his turtle wife
and his ten little turtle children
in a small mudhole
by the side of a pond.

They had everything
they needed
and they were very happy.
They had a smooth rock
in front of their door
to sunbathe on.

They had a water lily
to sit under
when they wanted
to sit in the shade.

They had a hollow log
that they rowed
around the pond
when they wanted
to visit their friends.

When they were hungry,
all they had to do
was open their mouths
and catch flies.

And for a very special treat,
Mrs. Turtle made shoo-fly pie.

The mudhole was so small

that at night

the ten little turtle children

slept stacked up like chairs,

one on top of the other.

"The one on the bottom

is a mud turtle,"

yelled the little turtle children

as they jumped into bed.

It was very cozy.

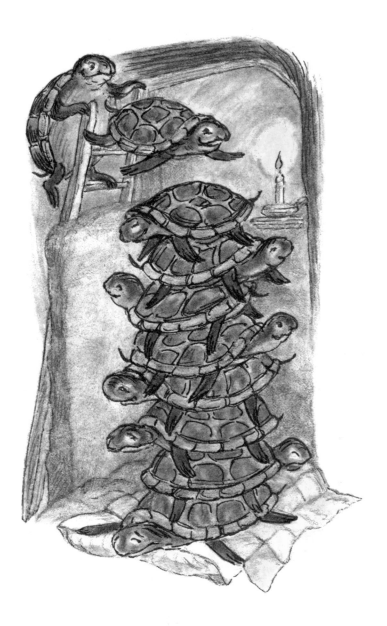

One day a new turtle
and his family
moved into
the mudhole
across the pond.

Right away
this turtle started
to make his
mudhole bigger.

He added another bedroom,
so that his children
didn't have to sleep stacked up.

He raked the pebbles
in front of his door.

He spread a towel
on the pebbles
to sunbathe on.

He put up
a large umbrella
so he could sit
in the shade
and sip a cool drink.

He had a shiny motor boat
that went putt-putt
all around the pond.

And when he was hungry,
his wife made shoo-fly pie,
and it wasn't even
a special treat.

The ten little turtle children
watched the new turtle children
play with their fancy water toys.

Mrs. Turtle watched
the new turtle's wife
lie under the umbrella
and sip a cool drink.

And Fred watched the new turtle

and his whole turtle family

get into the shiny motor boat.

It went putt-putting

around the pond,

making a lot of noise

and pollution.

Then some of the

ten little turtle children

started to complain.

"All I ever have

is hand-me-down toys,"

said the littlest turtle child.

And he threw his

dried pod-and-seed rattle

into the pond.

"All I have is a xylophone
made of old fish bones
that goes CHINK CHONK
instead of PLINK PLONK,"
cried the oldest boy turtle.
And he stamped on
his fish bone xylophone
till it couldn't chink chonk
or plink plonk anymore.

The oldest girl turtle

shook her head sadly and said,

"All I have is a jump rope

made of reeds

that gets tangled around my feet

every time I skip Hi-Lo Water."

And she began to cry.

Then all the

ten little turtle children

started to complain

about sleeping all stacked up.

"The one on the bottom

is a stick-in-the-mud turtle,"

they grumbled

as they fell

into bed.

And Mrs. Turtle said,

"If I had a washing machine
    like the new turtle's wife,
    I'd have time to make
    shoo-fly pie every day
    and not just for special treats."

But Fred didn't say anything.

He just opened his mouth

and caught another fly.

This made Mrs. Turtle so angry

that she said,

"Fred, you really are

a STICK-IN-THE-MUD turtle!"

One day the new turtle's wife

invited Fred's wife

and the children

over for a visit.

The ten little turtle children

lay on the towel in the sun,

and played with

the new turtle children

and their fancy water toys.

"Let's play Zap-Ball!"
yelled one of
the new turtle children.

He threw
a giant water ball
right at the
littlest turtle child . . .
ZAP!

It hit the littlest turtle child . . .

ZONK!

and he fell and hurt his toe.

"OW YOW!"

cried the littlest turtle child,

hopping around

on one foot.

"I want to play Submarine,"
screamed one of
the new turtle children.
He zoomed a torpedo
at the oldest boy turtle.
The torpedo hissed nastily
around and around
the oldest boy turtle's head.

He tried

to escape

by diving into

a pile of pebbles.

"Help! Help!" he yelled.

"Serves you right,"

said the new turtle child.

And he pulled the oldest

boy turtle's tail.

"Let's play

Miss Mermaid's Beauty Salon,"

said a new girl turtle.

"How do you play that?"

asked the oldest girl turtle.

"You'll see," said the new girl turtle.

And she tipped the water swan

that the oldest girl turtle

was floating on.

"GLUG, GLUG, GLUG,"

said the oldest girl turtle

as she fell in the water,

and all the curl

came out of her hair.

Mrs. Turtle was sitting

with the new turtle's wife

under the umbrella,

sipping a cool drink.

"Well," said the new turtle's wife,

"our children seem to be

getting along just fine."

"Oh my, yes," said Mrs. Turtle.

But just then the wind

blew the umbrella over.

It knocked Mrs. Turtle on the head,

and her drink spilled

all over her best dress.

"Never mind,"
  said the new turtle's wife.
"Let's go for a ride
  around the pond
  in the motor boat.
  You can introduce us
  to all your friends."
  So they jumped
  into the motor boat,
  and all the new turtle children
  hit and bit
  and pulled and punched.

And when they went
putt-putting around the pond,
they made so much noise
and so much smoke
that all Fred's family's friends
were frightened
and hopped into their holes
or flew away.

"Well, children,

   I think it is time to go home,"

   said Fred's wife.

"Thank you very much

   for a very nice visit,"

said the ten little turtle children.

When they got home,

Fred was sitting by the door

sunbathing on the smooth rock.

Fred's wife and his

ten little turtle children

sat down on the smooth rock

and sunbathed

with him.

When it got too hot,

they all sat in the shade

of the water lily

and felt the cool breeze.

The littlest turtle child

got some dried pods and seeds

and made a new rattle

that he decorated

with forget-me-nots.

The oldest boy turtle

put soft green moss

on his fish bone xylophone.

It went PLINK PLONK

ever so nicely.

The oldest girl turtle

braided daisies and violets

into her jump rope.

When she skipped

Hi-Lo Water,

her feet were covered

with flowers.

And the ten little turtle children
dipped their toes in the water
and played skip-hop-frog.
It was very cozy.

Then they all got into
their hollow log
and rowed around the pond.
Their friends came hopping
out of their holes
or flew down
from the branches
to visit them.

When they got home again,

Fred's wife went into

the kitchen

and baked *two* pies.

"This pie is all for you, Fred,"
said Mrs. Turtle.
"It's a very special treat.
It's called *super double*
shoo-fly pie."
Fred didn't say anything.
He just opened his mouth
and swallowed all of his
super double shoo-fly pie
at one gulp.

"Who is the other pie for?"
yelled the ten little
turtle children.
"Is it for us?"

"Yes," said Mrs. Turtle,

"it's for all of my

dear little ten little

turtle children."

"It's a super dooper

double delicious

shoo-fly pie,"

cried the ten

little turtle children.

And they gobbled it up.

Then the ten
little turtle children
jumped into bed
all stacked up
one on top of the other,
and Mrs. Turtle sang
a soft turtle lullaby to them.

"The one on the top
is a turtle dove,"
they murmured
as they fell asleep.
It was very cozy.